Richard Herne Shepherd

The Bibliography of Swinburne

a bibliographical list, arranged in chronological order, of the published

writings in verse and prose of Algernon Charles Swinburne

Richard Herne Shepherd

The Bibliography of Swinburne
a bibliographical list, arranged in chronological order, of the published writings in verse and prose of Algernon Charles Swinburne

ISBN/EAN: 9783337368951

Printed in Europe, USA, Canada, Australia, Japan

Cover: Foto ©Andreas Hilbeck / pixelio.de

More available books at **www.hansebooks.com**

THE

Bibliography of Swinburne

A BIBLIOGRAPHICAL LIST

ARRANGED IN CHRONOLOGICAL ORDER

OF THE

PUBLISHED WRITINGS IN VERSE AND PROSE

OF

ALGERNON CHARLES SWINBURNE

(1857-1887)

LONDON

GEORGE REDWAY

1887

NEW EDITION

REVISED AND CONSIDERABLY ENLARGED.

[*Only* 250 *copies printed.*]

PREFACE TO THE FOURTH EDITION.

BORN on April 5, 1837, in the year of Queen Victoria's accession, of which the whole nation is now celebrating the Jubilee, ALGERNON CHARLES SWINBURNE to-day attains the jubilee or fiftieth year of his own life, and may be therefore claimed as an essentially and exclusively Victorian poet. Of the half-century of life now completed, more than a quarter of a century has been devoted to fruitful and noble work in song and to work hardly less noble and fruitful in the field of criticism.

In issuing this new edition, revised throughout and brought down to date, of a bibliographical record originally published some four years ago, the Compiler cannot deny himself the pleasure of associating with the date the coincidence, not only of a double jubilee, but also of a double birthday.

Long distant may the day be when this record, already so goodly, can be made complete in a final sense, and collectors of the books of our greatest Victorian poet and critic be able to echo Lord Melbourne's callous expression of grateful relief that they can bind him up !

As on former occasions the Compiler invites the co-operation of literary correspondents and will be grateful to any one who will correct an error or supply an omission.

RICHARD HERNE SHEPHERD.

KINGSTON VALE,
April 5, 1887.

THE
𝕭ibliography of Swinburne.

1857-1858.

UNDERGRADUATE PAPERS. Oxford: W. Mansell, High-street ;
London : Whittaker and Co. 1857-1858, 8vo., pp. 186.

Edited by Mr. (now Professor) John Nichol (whose historical drama of
Hannibal was noticed by Mr. Swinburne, in 1872, in the *Fortnightly Review*).
The chief contributors were George Rankine Luke, the late T. H. Green,
Professor Albert Venn Dicey, Mr. George Birkbeck Hill (author of " Johnson
and his Circle "), and Algernon Charles Swinburne. Mr. Swinburne's contri-
butions, five in number, included a very amusing parody, *The Monomaniac's
Tragedy*, the first Canto of a poem entitled "Queen Yseult," a paper on
Marlowe and Webster, &c. &c.

CONGREVE, WILLIAM, short prose article, signed "A. C. S.," in
*The Imperial Dictionary of Universal Biography, a series of
original memoirs of distinguished men of all ages and all nations*,
edited by John Francis Waller, LL.D. London : William
Mackenzie [1857], vol i., p. 979.

An entirely different paper from that which appeared twenty years afterwards
(1877), over the same initials, in the Ninth Edition of the *Encyclopædia
Britannica.* (*Vide infra*, p. 24.)

1860-1861.

THE QUEEN-MOTHER. ROSAMOND. TWO PLAYS. BY ALGERNON
CHARLES SWINBURNE.   London : Basil Montagu Pickering.
1860.

Collation : Half-title, Title, Leaf of Dedication and of Persons represented
(in *The Queen Mother*), Half-title to *The Queen Mother*, pp. 217, and Leaf of
Errata.   Half-title to *Rosamond* between pages 160 and 161.

1862.

Contributions to *Once-a-Week*, 1862 :—

The Fratricide (Finnish).—Feb. 15 (vol. vi., pp. 215-216).

Dead Love (prose).   With an illustration by M. J. Lawless.—Oct. 11 (vol. vii., pp. 432-434).

"The Fratricide" was reprinted in *Poems and Ballads* (1866), pp. 329-333, under the title of "The Bloody Son."   "Dead Love" has never been reprinted.

Contributions to *The Spectator*, 1862 :—

A Song in Time of Order, 1852.—April 26, fol. 466.

Before Parting.—May 17, fol. 550.

After Death (Breton).*—May 24, fol. 578-9.

Faustine.—May 31, fol. 606-7.

Mr. George Meredith's *Modern Love* (Letter to the Editor).—June 7, fol. 632-3.

A Song in Time of Revolution, 1860.—June 28, fol. 718.

The Sundew.—July 26, fol. 830.

August.—Sept. 6, fol. 997.

Charles Baudelaire :   *Les Fleurs du Mal.*—Sept. 6, fol. 998-1000.

The seven poems were reprinted, without omission or alteration, in *Poems and Ballads* (1866), pp. 158-160 ; 212-213 ; 324-326 ; 122-129 ; 161-165 ; 214-216 ; 248-250.   The letter on Mr. George Meredith's *Modern Love* and the notice of Charles Baudelaire's *Fleurs du Mal* have not been reprinted.

---

* A footnote, not reprinted in *Poems and Ballads*, states these lines to be taken "from the *Recueil de Chants Bretons*, edited by Félicien Cossu, 1ère série (no more published), pp. 89, Paris, 1858."

1864.

THE CHILDREN OF THE CHAPEL. A Tale. By the author of "Mark Dennis." London : Joseph Masters. 1864, pp. 124.

The interludes in verse were contributed by A. C. SWINBURNE.

The authoress of the prose portion of the tale was Miss Gordon (now Mrs. Disney Leith), a cousin of the poet.

1865.

ATALANTA IN CALYDON. A TRAGEDY. By ALGERNON CHARLES SWINBURNE. London: Edward Moxon and Co. 1865, 4to. pp. xii. 111.

CHASTELARD; A TRAGEDY. By ALGERNON CHARLES SWINBURNE. London: Edward Moxon and Co. 1865, pp. viii. 219.

A Selection from the Works of Lord Byron. Edited and Prefaced by Algernon Charles Swinburne. London: Edward Moxon and Co. 1866, pp. xxxii. 244.

The Preface, dated "Christmas, 1865," is reprinted in *Essays and Studies* (1875), pp. 238-258.

1866.

Speech in answer to the toast of the "Imaginative Literature of England," at the Seventy-seventh Anniversary Dinner of the Royal Literary Fund, at Willis's Rooms, Wednesday, May 2, 1866.—*Report of the Anniversary*, p. 27.

POEMS AND BALLADS. By ALGERNON CHARLES SWINBURNE. London : Edward Moxon and Co. 1866, pp. vii. 344.

> The contents include sixty-two separate pieces, of which eight had been already published in 1862, in *The Spectator* and *Once-a-Week*, and fifty-four appear here for the first time.

NOTES ON POEMS AND REVIEWS. By ALGERNON CHARLES SWINBURNE. London : John Camden Hotten. 1866, 8vo., pp. 23.

⊬ Cleopatra. By Algernon Swinburne. With an illustration by Frederick Sandys.—*Cornhill Magazine*, September, 1866 (vol. xiv., pp. 331-333).

> This poem, which did not appear until after the publication of the first series of *Poems and Ballads*, has not been reprinted by the author in any of his subsequent collected volumes.

Cleopatra. A few copy in Pamphlet form.

1867.

A Song of Italy. By Algernon Charles Swinburne. London : John Camden Hotten. 1867, pp. 66.

Reprinted in *Songs of Two Nations* (1875).

Contributions to *The Fortnightly Review*, 1867 :—
Child's Song in Winter.—Jan. (n.s., vol. i., pp. 19-26.)

Reprinted (as the first of " Four Songs of Four Seasons, § Winter in Northumberland,") in *Poems and Ballads, Second Series* (1878), pp. 163-176.

Ode on the Insurrection in Candia.—March (vol. i., pp. 284-289).

Reprinted in *Songs before Sunrise* (1871), pp. 240-250.

Morris's " Life and Death of Jason."—July (vol. ii., pp. 19-28.)

Reprinted in *Essays and Studies* (1875), pp. 110-122.

Regret.—Sept. (vol. ii., p. 271.)

Reprinted, with considerable alterations, and with the addition of two stanzas, under the title of *Pastiche*, in *Poems and Ballads, Second Series* (1878), pp. 129-130.

Mr. Arnold's New Poems.—Oct. (vol. ii., pp. 414-445).

Reprinted in *Essays and Studies* (1875), pp. 123-183.

The Halt before Rome, September 1867.—Nov. (vol. ii., pp. 539-546).

Reprinted in *Songs before Sunrise* (1871), pp. 45-59.

A Lost Vigil.—Dec. (vol. ii., pp. 671-672).

Reprinted, under the title of " A Wasted Vigil," in *Poems and Ballads, Second Series* (1878), pp. 55-59.

An Appeal to England. —*Morning Star*, Friday, November 22, 1867.

Reprinted in *Songs before Sunrise* (1871), pp. 253-257.

1868.

WILLIAM BLAKE. A CRITICAL ESSAY. By ALGERNON CHARLES SWINBURNE. With illustrations from Blake's designs in facsimile. London : John Camden Hotten. 1868, pp. viii. 304.

NOTES ON THE ROYAL ACADEMY EXHIBITION, 1868. Part I. By W. M. ROSSETTI. Part. II. By ALGERNON C. SWINBURNE. London : John Camden Hotten. 1868, pp. iv. 51.

> Mr. Swinburne's contribution extends from page 31 to the end. When printed in *Essays and Studies*, 1875 (pp. 358-380), a sentence in the notice of Leighton's "Acme and Septimius" (p. 33), the entire notice of Millais (pp. 33-35), and the notice of a picture of "Mary Stuart about to sign her abdication" (containing a passage in blank verse which now forms part of a speech in the drama of *Mary Stuart*), pp. 37-39, were omitted.

SIENA. By ALGERNON CHARLES SWINBURNE. London : John Camden Hotten. 1868, pp. 15.

> Contributed to *Lippincott's Magazine* (Philadelphia), June, 1868 (vol. i., pp. 622-629), and published in a separate form in London, to secure the English copyright. Very few copies were printed, and still fewer issued. *(Pamphlet)* Reprinted in *Songs before Sunrise* (1871), pp. 191-204, where some of the prose notes which originally accompanied the poem do not reappear.

Contributions to *The Fortnightly Review*, 1868 :—
Ave atque Vale. In Memory of Charles Baudelaire.—January, 1868 (n.s., vol. iii., pp. 71-76).

> Reprinted in *Poems and Ballads, Second Series* (1878), pp. 71-83.

Notes on Designs of the Old Masters at Florence.—July (vol. iv., pp. 16-40).

> Reprinted in *Essays and Studies*, (1875), pp. 314-357.

A Watch in the Night.—December (vol. iv. pp. 618-622).

> Reprinted in *Songs before Sunrise* (1871), pp. 30-37.

1869.

Christabel and the Lyrical and Imaginative Poems of S. T. Coleridge. Arranged and introduced by Algernon Charles Swinburne. London : Sampson Low.   1869, pp. xxvii. 150.

The Introductory Essay is reprinted in *Essays and Studies* (1875), pp. 259 275.

Editors sub-edited.—Letter dated " Holmwood, Sept. 29, 1869," and signed " A. C. Swinburne," disavowing the authorship of a supplementary note at page 150 of the above volume.—*Athenæum*, October 9, 1869, p. 463.

Contributions to *The Fortnightly Review*, 1869 :—
Notes on the Text of Shelley.—May 1869 (n.s., vol. v., pp. 539-561).

Reprinted, with additions, in *Essays and Studies* (1875), pp. 184-237.

Victor Hugo : " L'Homme qui Rit."—July 1869 (n.s., vol. vi., pp. 73-81).

Reprinted in *Essays and Studies* (1875), pp. 1-16.

Victor Hugo and English Anonyms.   To the Editor of "The Daily Telegraph."—Letter (of nearly a column) dated " Oct. 21," and signed "Algernon Charles Swinburne."—*Daily Telegraph*, Friday, October 22, 1869, fol. 5. col. 6.

On the *Times'* review of *L'Homme qui Rit*, which appeared in the number for October 14, 1869.

Super Flumina Babylonis.—*Fortnightly Review*, October 1869 (n.s., vol. vi., pp. 386-389).

Reprinted in *Songs before Sunrise* (1871), pp. 38-44.

Intercession.   (Four Sonnets, dated " Paris, Sept., 1869.")— *Fortnightly Review*, November, 1869 (n.s., vol. vi., pp. 509-510).

Reprinted in *Songs of Two Nations* (1875), *Diræ* § xii., pp. 66-69.

/

1870.

Contributions to *The Fortnightly Review,* 1870 :—
The Complaint of Monna Lisa.   (Double sestina, *Decameron,* x. 7.)
—February 1870 (n.s., vol. vii., pp. 176-179).
Reprinted in *Poems and Ballads, Second Series* (1878), pp. 60-68.

The Poems of Dante Gabriel Rossetti.—May 1870 (n.s., vol. vii., pp. 551-579).
Reprinted in *Essays and Studies* (1875), pp. 60-109.

The Children of the Poor.   (From the French of Victor Hugo.) Translated by A. C. Swinburne.—*Cassell's Magazine,* London, May, 1870 (n.s., vol. i., p. 329).
Reprinted in *Poems and Ballads, Second Series* (1878), pp. 225-226.

ODE ON THE PROCLAMATION OF THE FRENCH REPUBLIC, September 4th, 1870.   By ALGERNON CHARLES SWINBURNE. London : F. S. Ellis.   1870, pp. 23.
Reprinted in *Songs of Two Nations* (1875).

1871.

SONGS BEFORE SUNRISE. By ALGERNON CHARLES SWINBURNE. London : F. S. Ellis. 1871, pp. viii. 287.

The contents include thirty-eight separate pieces (besides the Dedication to Joseph Mazzini), of which six had been previously published, and thirty-two appeared here for the first time.

Contributions to *The Dark Blue* :—
The End of a Month. With an illustration by Simeon Solomon.— April, 1871 (vol. i., pp. 217-220).

Reprinted, under the title of " At a Month's End," with an additional stanza, in the second series of *Poems and Ballads* (1878), pp. 37-45.

Simeon Solomon : Notes on his " Vision of Love," and other studies.—July, 1871 (vol. i., pp. 568-577).

Not included in Mr. Swinburne's collected *Essays and Studies* or prose *Miscellanies.*

Tristram and Iseult : Prelude of an Unfinished Poem.—*Pleasure : A Holiday Book of Prose and Verse.* London : Henry S. King and Co. 1871, pp. 45-52.

Reprinted, with some verbal alterations, in *Tristram of Lyonesse and other Poems* (1882), pp. 3-11.

John Ford.—*Fortnightly Review*, July 1871 (n.s., vol. x., pp. 42-63).

Reprinted in *Essays and Studies* (1875), pp. 276-313.

1872.

UNDER THE MICROSCOPE. By ALGERNON CHARLES SWINBURNE. London : David White.   1872, pp. 88.

Not republished, either separately, or in the author's collected *Essays and Studies* or prose *Miscellanies.*

Sestina.—*Once-a-Week.*   New Series.   January 6, 1872 (vol. ix., p. 1).

Reprinted in *Poems and Ballads, Second Series* (1878), pp. 46-48.

Contributions to *The Fortnightly Review*, 1872 :—
Victor Hugo : " L'Année Terrible."—September, 1872 (n.s., vol. xii., pp. 243-267).

Reprinted in *Essays and Studies* (1875), pp. 17-59.

Mr. John Nichol's " Hannibal : A Historical Drama."—December 1872 (n.s., vol. xii., pp. 751-753).

Not included in either of Mr. Swinburne's collected volumes of *Essays and Studies* or *Miscellanies.*

1873.

LE TOMBEAU DE THÉOPHILE GAUTIER.   Paris : Alphonse Lemerre, Editeur.   1873, pp. ii. 179.   .

> Mr. Swinburne's contributions to this volume are six in number :—1. Sonnet
> with a copy of "Mademoiselle de Maupin." 2. Memorial Verses on the Death
> of Théophile Gautier [published also in *The Fortnightly Review*, January
> 1873, n.s., vol. xiii. pp. 68-73]. 3. Ode : "Quelle fleur, ô mort, quel joyau,
> quel chant." 4. Sonnet : "Pour mettre une couronne au front d'une chanson."
> 5. In obitum Theophili Poetæ Clarissimi. 6. Επιγραμματα Επιτυμβιδια ιις Θεςφιλον
> (pp. 155-172).   The English, French and Latin contributions are reprinted in
> *Poems and Ballads, Second Series* (1878), pp. 84-97, 230-236 ; but the Greek
> verses do not reappear.

North and South.—*Fortnightly Review*, May 1873 (n.s., vol. xiii.,
pp. 564-566).

> Reprinted, under the title of "Relics," in *Poems and Ballads, Second Series*
> (1878), pp. 32-36.

DIRÆ : Twenty Sonnets.—*Examiner*, March 22 to June 14, 1873 :
pp. 307, 332, 362, 386, 410, 433, 458, 482, 519, 543, 568*, 589,
615.

> These Sonnets, together with four others from *The Fortnightly Review*,
> were republished as the third section of *Songs of Two Nations* (1875).

Mr. Swinburne's Sonnets in *The Examiner*.   To the Editor of *The
Spectator*.   Letter dated "Ball. Coll., Oxford, May 25, 1873,"
and signed "A. C. Swinburne."—*Spectator*, May 31, 1873, fol.
697.

Christianity and Imperialism.   By A. C. Swinburne.—*Examiner*,
June 7, 1873, pp. 585-586.

---

* This number (for May 31, 1873) contains extracts from a letter of Mr. Swinburne to the editor.

1874.

Sonnet.   To Victor Hugo.—*Athenæum*, January 3, 1874 (p. 20).

Reprinted in *Poems and Ballads, Second Series* (1878), p. 107.

Contributions to the *Fortnightly Review*, 1874 :—
The Year of the Rose.—August, 1874 (n.s., vol. xvi., pp. 201-203).

Reprinted in *Poems and Ballads, Second Series* (1878), pp. 49-54.

In Memory of Barry Cornwall (October 4, 1874).—November, 1874 (n.s., vol. xvi., pp. 659-660).

Reprinted in *Poems and Ballads, Second Series* (1878), pp. 100-103.

Barry Cornwall. Four stanzas of six lines each. (With note to B. W. Procter, dated " Sept. 1, 1868," and signed " Algernon C. Swinburne.")—*Pall Mall Gazette*, October 20, 1874, p. 11.

Reprinted, under the title of *Youth and Age* (but without the accompanying note), in *Poems and Ballads, Second Series* (1878), pp. 98-99.

BOTHWELL : A TRAGEDY. By ALGERNON CHARLES SWINBURNE. London : Chatto and Windus. 1874. pp. viii. 532.

Dedicated, in a French sonnet, to Victor Hugo.

Walter Savage Landor. Twenty-one lines of Latin verse.—*Academy*, December 12, 1874 (p. 634).

Reprinted in *Poems and Ballads, Second Series* (1878), pp. 237-238, under the title of *Ad Catullum*.

" Love laid his sleepless head."—Song, four stanzas of four lines each.—Printed in *The Examiner*, December 26, 1874 (and in other daily and weekly journals).   Published separately, with music by Arthur Sullivan (Boosey and Co.), pp. 5, 4to., and again with music by Hastings Crossley (Novello, Ewer and Co.), 4to., pp. 5.

Reprinted in *Poems and Ballads, Second Series* (1878), pp. 133-134.

1875.

GEORGE CHAPMAN: A CRITICAL ESSAY. By ALGERNON CHARLES SWINBURNE. London: Chatto and Windus. 1875, pp. 187.

Written, and originally published, as an Introduction to the first collected Edition of The Works of George Chapman, including his Plays, Poems, Translation of Homer, and Minor Translations, in three volumes, edited by Richard Herne Shepherd, and published by Chatto and Windus (London, 1874-1875). Mr. Swinburne's "Essay on the Poetical and Dramatic Works of George Chapman" was prefixed to the volume of "Poems and Minor Translations" (1875), where it occupies pp. ix. to lxxi. of the preliminary matter.

Mr. Swinburne and his Critics.—Letter to the Editor of *The Examiner*, dated "3, Great James-street, April 3, 1875," and signed "A. C. Swinburne."—*Examiner*, April 10, 1875 (p. 408).

Contributions to the *Fortnightly Review*, 1875 :—
A Vision of Spring in Winter.—April 1875 (n.s., vol. xvii., pp. 505-507).

Reprinted in *Poems and Ballads, Second Series* (1878), pp. 135-140.

The Three Stages of Shakespeare.—May, 1875 (n.s., vol. xvii., pp. 613-632) ; January 1876 (vol. xix., pp. 24-45).

Reprinted, with additions, in *A Study of Shakespeare* (1880).

"The Society for the Suppression of Vice."—Letter to the Editor of *The Athenæum*, dated "3, Great James-street, May 26, 1875," and signed "A. C. Swinburne."—*Athenæum*, May 29, 1875 (p. 720).

At Parting.—*Athenæum*, August 7, 1875 (p. 181).

Reprinted in *Poems and Ballads, Second Series* (1878), pp. 144-145.

ESSAYS AND STUDIES. By ALGERNON CHARLES SWINBURNE. London : Chatto and Windus. 1875, pp. xii. 380.

CONTENTS :—Preface. 1. Victor Hugo, *L'Homme qui Rit*. 2. *L'Année Terrible*. 3. Poems of Dante Gabriel Rossetti. 4. Morris's Life and Death of

Jason.   5. Matthew Arnold's New Poems.   6. Notes on the Text of Shelley.
7. Byron. 8. Coleridge. 9. John Ford. 10. Notes on Designs of the Old
Masters at Florence.   11. Notes on some Pictures of 1868.
The Preface alone is new; but there are addenda and footnotes to some of
the reprinted essays; notably to those on Shelley and Byron.

SONGS OF TWO NATIONS.   By ALGERNON CHARLES SWINBURNE.
I. A Song of Italy.   II. Ode on the Proclamation of the French
Republic.   III. Diræ.   London: Chatto and Windus.   1875,
pp. viii. 78.

The two introductory stanzas in italic between the Title and Contents are
new: the first and second divisions of the volume had been previously published, in a separate form, and the third division, *Diræ*, in the *Examiner* and
Fortnightly Review.

† Auguste Vacquerie: *Aujourd'hui et Demain.—Examiner*, November 6, 1875 (fol. 1247-1250).

Reprinted in Swinburne's *Miscellanies* (1886).

The Edgar Poe Memorial.   Letter to Miss Sara S. Rice, dated
"Holmwood, Nov. 9, 1875," and signed "A. C. Swinburne."—
Facsimiled in *Edgar Allan Poe: A Memorial Volume.   By Sara
Sigourney Rice.*   4to.   Baltimore: Turnbull Brothers, 1877.

Epitaph on a Slanderer.—*Examiner*, November 20, 1875 (fol.
1304).

Not reprinted in any subsequent collected volume.

Beaumont and Fletcher.—*Encyclopædia Britannica.   Ninth Edition.*
Vol. III.   Edinburgh: Adam and Charles Black.   1875, pp.
469-474.

The Devil's Due.   Letter relating to Mr. Robert Buchanan and
the authorship of *Jonas Fisher.*   Signed "Thomas Maitland, St.
Kilda, December 28, 1875."—*Examiner*, December 11, 1875
(fol. 1388).

This letter gave rise to an action for libel by Mr. Robert Buchanan against
Mr. P. A. Taylor, M.P., the proprietor of *The Examiner*, tried in the Court
of Common Pleas, June 29-30, and July 1, 1876.   The letter was read during
the trial, and its authorship admitted.

*Auguste Vacquerie. Par Swinburne. Paris
Michel Lévy frères Éditeurs.
Rue Aubert 3. Place De l'Opéra.
Libraire Nouvelle
Boulevards des Italiens 15 au coin de la Rue 4
1875.
8vo. pp 27. (Campbell) in french.*

1876.

Two Leaders (Two Sonnets).—*Athenæum*, January 8, 1876 (p. 54).
Reprinted in *Poems and Ballads, Second Series* (1878), pp. 155-156.

Joseph and his Brethren. A Dramatic Poem. By Charles Wells.
With an Introduction by Algernon Charles Swinburne. London :
Chatto and Windus. 1876.
Mr. Swinburne's Introduction is substantially identical, save for the omission
of the extracts, with his article in *The Fortnightly Review* entitled " An Un-
known Poet" (February 1875, n. s., vol. xvii., pp. 217-232).

A Discovery.—*Athenæum*, January 15, 1876 (p. 87).

" King Henry VIII.," and the Ordeal by Metre. Letter dated
" Holmwood, Jan. 10, 1876," and signed "A. C. Swinburne."—
Academy, January 15, 1876 (pp. 53-55).

Sir Henry Taylor's Lyrics. Letter dated " Holmwood, Jan. 22,
1876," and signed "A. C. Swinburne."—*Academy*, January 29,
1876 (p. 98).

A Birth Song (for Olivia Frances Madox Rossetti, born Sept. 20,
1875).—*Athenæum*, February 19, 1876 (pp. 263-264).
Reprinted in *Poems and Ballads, Second Series* (1878), pp. 110-115.

Nocturne.—Six stanzas of six lines each, and Envoi of three lines,
signed "Algernon Charles Swinburne." (With prose letter, also

in French, to Stéphane Mallarmé, dated " Holmwood, Henley-on-Thames, janvier 1876," and signed "A. C. Swinburne."—*La République des Lettres, Revue Mensuelle* (Paris: Alphonse Derenne, Editeur, 52 Boulevard Saint-Michel), Troisième livraison, février 20, 1876 (pp. 79-80).

Reprinted, but without the accompanying letter, in *Poems and Ballads, Second Series* (1878), pp. 227-229.

ERECHTHEUS: A TRAGEDY. By ALGERNON CHARLES SWINBURNE. London: Chatto and Windus. 1876, pp. viii. 107.

Report of the First Anniversary Meeting of the Newest Shakespeare Society (April 1, 1876).—*Examiner*, April 1, 1876 (fol. 381-383).

The Newest Shakespeare Society: Additions and Corrections. (Signed "Chimaera Bombinans in Vacuo.")—*Examiner*, April 15, 1876 (fol. 440-441).

Reprinted in the Appendix to *A Study of Shakespeare* (1880), pp. 275 to end.

The Last Oracle. (A.D. 361.)—*Belgravia*, May, 1876 (vol. xxix., pp. 329-332.

Reprinted in *Poems and Ballads, Second Series* (1878), pp. 1-9.

Charles Lamb's Letters to Godwin.—Letter to the Editor of *The Athenæum*, dated "3, Great James-street, Bedford-row."—*Athenæum*, May 13, 1876 (p. 664).

Epicede. (James Lorimer Graham).—*Athenæum*, June 10, 1876 (p. 794).

Reprinted in *Poems and Ballads, Second Series* (1878), pp. 104-106.

A Song in Season.—*Belgravia*, July, 1876 (vol. xxx., pp. 5-9).

Reprinted in *Poems and Ballads, Second Series* (1878), pp. 146-154.

A Forsaken Garden.—*Athenæum*, July 22, 1876 (p. 112).

Reprinted in *Poems and Ballads, Second Series* (1878), pp. 27-31.

A Ballad of Dreamland.—*Belgravia*, September, 1876 (vol. xxx., p. 324).

Reprinted in *Poems and Ballads, Second Series* (1878), pp. 123-124.

Mr. Forman's Edition of Shelley.—*Academy*, November 25, 1876 (p. 520).

George Chapman.—*Encyclopædia Britannica*. Ninth Edition, vol. v. Edinburgh, 1876 (pp. 396-397).

NOTE OF AN ENGLISH REPUBLICAN ON THE MUSCOVITE CRUSADE. By ALGERNON CHARLES SWINBURNE. London : Chatto and Windus. 1876, pp. 24.

1877.

William Congreve.—*Encyclopædia Britannica.*   Ninth Edition, vol. vi.   Edinburgh, 1877 (pp. 271-272).

The "Ode to a Nightingale."—Letter to the Editor of *The Athenæum*, signed "A. C. Swinburne."—*Athenæum*, January 27, 1877 (p. 117).

Ballad against the Enemies of France.   By François Villon. (Translated and endorsed by A. C. Swinburne, 1876.)—*Athenæum*, February 17, 1877 (p. 224).

> Reprinted in *Poems and Ballads, Second Series* (1878), pp. 212-214.

Victor Hugo: "La Sieste de Jeanne."   Letter dated "Feb. 17, 1877."—*Athenæum*, February 24, 1877 (p. 257).

The Sailing of the Swallow.—*Gentleman's Magazine*, March 1877 (pp. 287-308).

> Reprinted in 1882, as the First Canto of *Tristram of Lyonesse*, in the volume bearing that title, pp. 13-40.

"Poems and Ballads."—Two notes on a misstatement in a London bookseller's catalogue, respecting the original edition of "Poems and Ballads," published by Moxon and Co. in 1866.—*Athenæum*, March 10 and 24, 1877 (pp. 319-320; 383).

"The Court of Love."—Letter dated "March 31, 1877," and signed "A. C. Swinburne."—*Athenæum*, April 14, 1877 (pp. 481-482).

Ex-Voto.—*Athenæum*, June 2, 1877 (p. 703).

Reprinted in *Poems and Ballads, Second Series* (1878), pp. 116-122.

Note on the words "irremeable" and "perdurable."—*Pall Mall Gazette*, June 15, 1877.

Note on a Question of the Hour.—*Athenæum*, June 16, 1877 (p. 768).

A protest against the publication of *L'Assommoir*, by M. Emile Zola, in the pages of *La République des Lettres*.

The Dispute of the Soul and Body of François Villon. Translated by A. C. Swinburne.—*Athenæum*, July 7, 1877 (p. 15).

Reprinted (with the word "soul" changed to "heart"), in *Poems and Ballads, Second Series* (1878), pp. 215-218.

A Ballad of François Villon, Prince of all Ballad-makers.—*Athenæum*, September 15, 1877 (p. 337).

Reprinted in *Poems and Ballads, Second Series* (1878), pp. 126-128.

A NOTE ON CHARLOTTE BRONTË. By ALGERNON CHARLES SWINBURNE. London: Chatto and Windus, 1877, pp. 97.

A YEAR'S LETTERS. By Mrs. Horace Manners.—*The Tatler*, August 25 to December 29, 1877.

A novelette, in the form of letters, not hitherto republished in a separate form.

Last Words of the "Agamemnon."—Undated note signed "A. C. Swinburne."—*Athenæum*, Nov. 10, 1877, p. 597.

1878.

Sonnets : The White Czar (two Sonnets, with Introductory note in prose) ; Rizpah ; To Louis Kossuth.—*Glasgow University Magazine*, February 1878 (no. ii., p. 17).

Reprinted in *Poems and Ballads, Second Series*, pp. 189-193.

"Love, Death, and Reputation."—(Note on a piece in Lamb's *Poetry for Children.*)—*Athenæum*, February 2, 1878 (p. 156).

Note on a Passage in Shelley (*Prometheus Unbound*, act iii., sc. i., l. 40).—*Athenæum*, February 9, 1878 (p. 188).

POEMS AND BALLADS. SECOND SERIES. By ALGERNON CHARLES SWINBURNE. London : Chatto and Windus. 1878, pp. ix. 240.

The contents include fifty-eight separate pieces. Of these thirty-six had been previously published, during the preceding eleven years, in various periodicals, as already indicated : the remaining twenty-two appear here for the first time.

1879.

Note on the Historical Play of King Edward III.—*Gentleman's Magazine*, August and September, 1879 (pp. 170-181 ; 330-349).

Reprinted as Appendix I. to *A Study of Shakespeare* (1880), pp. 231-274.

1880.

A STUDY OF SHAKESPEARE. By ALGERNON CHARLES SWIN-
BURNE. London : Chatto and Windus. 1880, pp. viii. 309.

A *Study of Shakespeare* had partly appeared in *The Fortnightly Review.*
Two pieces, reprinted in the Appendix—1. Note on the Historical Play of
King Edward the Third ; 2. Report of the Proceedings on the First Anniversary
Session of the Newest Shakespeare Society—had appeared in *The Gentleman's
Magazine* and *The Examiner* respectively.

Mr. Swinburne's "Study of Shakespeare." (Note dated "Jan. 3,
1880," on a criticism by Prof. Dowden.)—*Academy*, January 10,
1880 (p. 28).

SONGS OF THE SPRINGTIDES. By ALGERNON CHARLES SWIN-
BURNE. London : Chatto and Windus. 1880, p. viii. 135.

CONTENTS :—Dedication to Edward John Trelawny. 2. Thalassius. 3.
On the Cliffs. 4. The Garden of Cymodoce. 5. Birthday Ode for the
Anniversary Festival of Victor Hugo, February 26, 1880. 6. Sonnet "On the
proposed desecration of Westminster Abbey by the erection of a monument to
the son of Napoleon III."

William Collins.—*The English Poets: Selections, with Critical In-
troductions by various writers, edited by Thomas Humphry Ward.*
London : Macmillan and Co. 1880, vol. iii., pp. 278-282.

Reprinted in Swinburne's *Miscellanies,* 1886.

Victor Hugo : "Religions et Religion."—*Fortnightly Review,* June,
1880 (n.s., vol. xxvii., pp. 761-768).

Letter signed "Algernon Charles Swinburne."—*Academy,* July 3,
1880.

Sonnet on the Refusal of the Amnesty by the French Senate. (July 14, 1880.)—*Fortnightly Review*, August 1880 (n.s., vol. xxviii., p. 199).

Reprinted in *Studies in Song* (1880), pp. 137-138.

Specimens of Modern Poets.

THE HEPTALOGIA, OR THE SEVEN AGAINST SENSE. A CAP WITH SEVEN BELLS.—1. The Higher Pantheism in a Nutshell. 2. John Jones. 3. The Poet and the Woodlouse. 4. The Person of the House (Idyl ccclxvi.). 5. Last Words of a Seventh-rate Poet. 6. Sonnet for a Picture. 7. Nephelidia.—London : Chatto and Windus. 1880, pp. 102.

A Century of English Poetry.—*Fortnightly Review*, October, 1880 (n.s., vol. xxviii., pp. 422-437).

A Relic of Dryden.—*Gentleman's Magazine*, October, 1880 (pp. 416-423).

The above two prose papers are reprinted in Swinburne's *Miscellanies* (1886).

Grand Chorus of Birds from Aristophanes, attempted in English after the original metre.—*Athenæum*, October 30, 1880 (p. 568).

Reprinted in *Studies in Song* (1880), pp. 67-74.

Short Notes on English Poets : Chaucer ; Spenser ; The Sonnets of Shakespeare ; Milton.—*Fortnightly Review*, December, 1880 (vol. xxviii., pp. 708-721).

Reprinted in Swinburne's *Miscellanies*, 1886.

Note (in French) on a passage in Lord Beaconsfield's "Endymion." —*Le Rappel* (Paris newspaper).

Reprinted in *The Pall Mall Gazette*, December 6, 1880.

STUDIES IN SONG. By ALGERNON CHARLES SWINBURNE. London : Chatto and Windus. 1880, pp. 212.

CONTENTS:—1. Song for the Centenary of Walter Savage Landor (with Dedication to Mrs. Lynn Linton). 2. Grand Chorus of Birds from Aristophanes. 3. Off Shore. 4. After Nine Years. 5. For a Portrait of Felice Orsini. 6. Evening on the Broads. 7. The Emperor's Progress. 8. The Resurrection of Alcilia. 9. The Fourteenth of July. 10. The Launch of the *Livadia*. 11. Six Years Old. 12. A Parting Song. 13. By the North Sea.

1881.

Mr. Swinburne's New Volume.—Note dated "Jan. 7, 1881," and signed "A. C. Swinburne."—*Academy*, January 15, 1881.

On the *Academy* reviewer's misquotation of a passage in Mr. Swinburne's *Studies in Song*, p. 143.

Tennyson and Musset.—*Fortnightly Review*, February, 1881 (n.s., vol. xxix. pp. 129-153).

Reprinted in Swinburne's *Miscellanies*, 1886.

Carlyle.—Letter (in French) to the Editor of the *Rappel.—Le Rappel* (Paris), février 19, 1881.

The Deaths of Thomas Carlyle and George Eliot. (Sonnet.)— *Athenæum*, April 30, 1881 (p. 591).

Reprinted in *Tristram of Lyonesse, and other Poems* (1882), p. 213.

Euthanatos. (Nine stanzas of seven lines each, dated "Feb. 4, 1881.")—*Athenæum*, June 11, 1881 (p. 782).

Reprinted in *Tristram of Lyonesse, and other Poems* (1882), pp. 231-233.

Seven Years Old. (Seven stanzas of seven lines each.)—*Athenæum*, August 20, 1881 (pp. 238-239).

Lines on the Death of Edward John Trelawny (dated "August 17, 1881 ").—*Athenæum*, August 27, 1881 (p. 275).

The Statue of Victor Hugo.—*Gentleman's Magazine*, September, 1881 (pp. 284-290).

The above three pieces are reprinted in *Tristram of Lyonesse, and other Poems* (1882).

MARY STUART. A TRAGEDY. By ALGERNON CHARLES SWIN-BURNE. London : Chatto and Windus. 1881, pp. viii., 203.

A short passage in this tragedy was originally published in Mr. Swinburne's *Notes on the Royal Academy Exhibition* (Hotten, 1868), pp. 37-39.

Disgust : A Dramatic Monologue.—*Fortnightly Review*, December, 1881 (n.s., vol. xxx., pp. 715-717).

A parody of *Despair: a Dramatic Monologue*, by the Poet Laureate, which appeared in *The Nineteenth Century* of the previous month.

1882.

Note on the Character of Mary Queen of Scots.—*Fortnightly Review,* January, 1882 (n.s., vol. xxxi., pp. 13-25).

Reprinted in Swinburne's *Miscellanies* (1886).

Sir William Gomm.   (Two Sonnets, dated "December, 1881.")— *Athenæum,* January 7, 1882 (p. 16).

On the Russian Persecution of the Jews.   (Sonnet, dated "Jan. 23, 1882.")—*Daily Telegraph,* Wednesday, January 25, 1882.

Three Sonnets. Bismarck at Canossa. (December 31, 1881.) Quia Nominor Leo.   (January, 1882.)—*Fortnightly Review,* February, 1882 (n.s., vol. xxxi., p. 155).

The above six sonnets are reprinted in *Tristram of Lyonesse, and other Poems* (1882), pp. 224-230.

John Keats.—Walter Savage Landor.—*Encyclopædia Britannica,* Ninth Edition, vol. xiv. (Edinburgh, 1882), pp. 22-24 ; 278-280.

After looking into Carlyle's *Reminiscences.*   Two Sonnets.—First printed in *Sonnets of Three Centuries : A Selection including many examples hitherto unpublished. Edited by T. Hall Caine.* London : Elliot Stock, 1882, 4to. (pp. 208-209).

Reprinted, with an important alteration in the second Sonnet, in *Tristram of Lyonesse, and other Poems* (1882), pp. 214-215.

TRISTRAM OF LYONESSE, AND OTHER POEMS. By ALGERNON CHARLES SWINBURNE. London : Chatto and Windus. 1882, pp. xi. 361.

Of *Tristram of Lyonesse* the Prelude and the first Canto had already appeared : of the minor poems thirteen had already appeared and the rest appear here for the first time.

1883.

Christopher Marlowe, }
Mary Queen of Scots. }
Encyclopædia Britannica, Ninth Edition, vol. xv. (Edinburgh, 1883),
pp. 556-558 ; 594-602.

> The article on "Mary Queen of Scots" is reprinted in Swinburne's
> *Miscellanies*, 1886.

Love and Scorn.   (Three Sonnets.)   *Athenæum*, January 6, 1883
(p. 16).

> Reprinted in *A Midsummer Holiday and other Poems* (1884), pp. 139-141.

The Death of Richard Wagner.—Printed in *The Musical Review,
A Weekly Musical Journal* (London), February 24, 1883 (vol. i.,
p. 128).

> Reprinted, with two slight verbal alterations or corrections, in *A Century
> of Roundels* (1883), p. 28.

A Coincidence.   (Note on Mr. A. H. Bullen's edition of the tragedy
of "Sir John van Olden Barnavelt.")—*Athenæum*, March 10,
1883.

La Question irlandaise.   Letter (in French) dated "Londres, 21
mars 1883," and signed * * *.—*Le Rappel* (Paris), Lundi, 26
mars, 1883.

"Marzo Pazzo."—*Academy*, March 31, 1883 (p. 220).

> Reprinted in *A Century of Roundels*, p. 83.

"Formosa." Par Auguste Vacquerie.—*Academy*, May 5, 1883 (p. 303).

Reprinted in Swinburne's *Miscellanies*, 1886.

Louis Blanc : Three Sonnets to his Memory.—*Fortnightly Review*, June, 1883 (pp. 765-766).

Reprinted in *A Midsummer Holiday and other Poems* (1884), pp. 125-127.

A Rondel—"At Sea." Signed "A. C. Swinburne."—*Musical Review*, June 2, 1883 (vol. i., p. 351).

Reprinted, with a verbal alteration or correction, in *A Century of Roundels*. p. 64.

Emily Brontë.—*Athenæum*, June 16, 1883 (pp. 762-763).

Reprinted in Swinburne's *Miscellanies*, 1886.

A CENTURY OF ROUNDELS. By ALGERNON CHARLES SWINBURNE. London : Chatto and Windus. 1883, small 4to., pp. xi. 100.

Six copies of this book were printed on hand-made paper, for gifts only and not for sale. Mr. Joseph Knight, writing in *Le Livre, Revue du Monde Littéraire*, Paris, octobre 1883, p. 617, says : —" J'ai la bonne fortune de posséder un des six exemplaires sur papier de choix, et je m'en félicite vivement."

Les Casquettes.—*English Illustrated Magazine*, October, 1883. (London, Macmillan and Co.), vol. i. pp. 16-21.

Reprinted, under the amended title of "Les Casquets," in *A Midsummer Holiday and other Poems* (1884), pp. 70-83.

Les Cenci. Drame de Shelley. Traduction de Tola Dorian, avec Preface de Algernon Charles Swinburne. Paris : Alphonse Lemerre, Editeur, 1883, pp. xviii. 129.

Victor Hugo : "La Légende des Siècles."—*Fortnightly Review*, October, 1883 (n.s., vol. xxxiv., pp. 497-520).

Reprinted in *A Study of Victor Hugo*. Lond. 1886, pp. 107-148.

Vos Deos Laudamus : The Tory Journalist's Anthem.—*Pall Mall Gazette*, Monday, December 17, 1883 (p. 4).

Reprinted, with the word "Tory" altered to "Conservative," in *A Midsummer Holiday and other Poems* (1884), pp. 128-131.

C

Dolorida.—Two stanzas in French, of four lines each, signed "Algernon Charles Swinburne."

Privately printed, as a fly-sheet of four pages, with the half-title, "In the Album of Adah Menken." Printed also in *Walnuts and Wine: a Christmas Annual, edited by Augustus M. Moore,* 1883, p. 3. In spite of Mr. Swinburne's apparent disclaimer in the *Pall Mall Gazette* of December 28, 1883, the lines are indubitably his, and are still extant, in his autograph and over his signature, in the Album referred to.

On the Death of Richard Doyle. (Sonnet.)—*Athenæum,* December 29, 1883, p. 865.

Reprinted in *A Midsummer Holiday and other Poems* (1884), p. 142.

1884.

Post Mortem. (Four Sonnets.)—*Fortnightly Review*, January, 1884 (n.s., vol. xxxv., pp. 65-66).

> Reprinted, under the title of "In Sepulcretis," in *A Midsummer Holiday and other Poems* (1884), pp. 134-138.

Near Cromer. (Sonnet.)—*Home Chimes.* London : January 2, 1884 (vol. i., p. 8).

> Reprinted, under the title of "A Solitude," in *A Midsummer Holiday and other Poems* (1884), p. 144.

Steele or Congreve? Four letters to the Editor of *The Spectator*, signed "A. C. Swinburne."—*Spectator*, March 29, April 5, 12, and 26, 1884, foll. 411, 441, 486, 550.

Wordsworth and Byron.—*Nineteenth Century*, April and May, 1884 (vol. xv., pp. 583-609 ; 764-790).

> Reprinted (with the omission of a parenthetical passage about Richardson's *Pamela*, occurring at pp. 592-593,) in Swinburne's *Miscellanies*, 1886.

Thanksgiving.—*Home Chimes*, June 14, 1884 (vol. i., p. 331).

> Reprinted, under the title of "Maytime in Midwinter," in *A Midsummer Holiday and other Poems* (1884), pp. 100-104.

On a Country Road.—*Nineteenth Century*, July, 1884 (vol. xvi., pp. 1-2).

> Reprinted in *A Midsummer Holiday* (1884), pp. 9-11.

A Ballad of Sark.—*English Illustrated Magazine*, August, 1884 (vol. i., p. 693).

"Clear the Way!"—*Pall Mall Gazette*, Tuesday, August 19, 1884 (p. 4).

The above two poems are reprinted in *A Midsummer Holiday and other Poems* (1884), pp. 84-86; 153-155.

Charles Reade.—*Nineteenth Century*, October, 1884 (vol. xvi., pp. 550-567).

Reprinted in Swinburne's *Miscellanies*, 1886.

A Midsummer Holiday and Other Poems. By Algernon Charles Swinburne.   London : Chatto and Windus, 1884, pp. vi. 189.

Contents :—A Midsummer Holiday.—1. The Seaboard ; 2. A Haven; 3. On a Country Road ; 4. The Mill Garden ; 5. A Sea-mark ; 6. The Cliff-side Path ; 7. In the Water ; 8. The Sunbows ; 9. On the Verge ; A New Year Ode ; Lines on the Monument of Giuseppe Mazzini ; Les Casquets; A Ballad of Sark ; Nine Years Old ; After a Reading ; Maytime in Midwinter ; A Double Ballad of August ; Heartsease Country ; A Ballad of Appeal ; Cradle Songs ; Pelagius ; Louis Blanc ; Vos Deos Laudamus ; On the Bicentenary of Corneille ; In Sepulcretis ; Love and Scorn; On the Death of Richard Doyle ; In Memory of Henry A. Bright ; A Solitude ; Victor Hugo ; L'Archipel de la Manche ; The Twilight of the Lords ; Clear the Way ! A Word for the Country ; A Word for the Nation ; A Word from the Psalmist ; A Ballad at Parting.

Eleven of the thirty-seven pieces contained in this volume had been previously published in various magazines and journals, as indicated above.

1885.

Charles Lamb and George Wither.—*Nineteenth Century*, January, 1885 (vol. xvii., pp. 66-91).

Reprinted in Swinburne's *Miscellanies*, 1886.

MARINO FALIERO. A TRAGEDY. By ALGERNON CHARLES SWINBURNE. London : Chatto and Windus, 1885, pp. viii. 151.

The Dedication, to Aurelio Saffi, is in nine rhymed stanzas of eight lines each. The Tragedy is in five Acts, and in blank verse, with the exception of the stanzas of the rhymed Latin chant or hymn intercalated in the Fourth and Fifth Acts.

The Work of Victor Hugo.—*Nineteenth Century*, July and August, 1885 (vol. xviii., pp. 14-29 ; 294-311).

Reprinted, with additions, in *A Study of Victor Hugo*, Lond. 1886, pp. 1-106.

The Interpreters. A Poem.—*English Illustrated Magazine*, October, 1885 (vol. iii., pp. 3-4).

1886.

Thomas Middleton.—*Nineteenth Century*, January, 1886 (vol. xix., pp. 138-153).

"The Best Hundred Books."—Two letters, signed "A. C. Swinburne."—*Pall Mall Gazette*, Tuesday, January 26, and Wednesday, January 27, 1886.

To Richard F. Burton. On his Translation of the "Arabian Nights." (Sonnet.)—*Athenæum*, February 6, 1886 (p. 199).

On the Death of Sir Henry Taylor. (Sonnet).—*Athenæum*, April 10, 1886 (p. 488).

A STUDY OF VICTOR HUGO. By ALGERNON CHARLES SWINBURNE. London : Chatto and Windus, 1886, pp. vi. 148.

The substance of the earlier and larger division of this volume, entitled "The Work of Victor Hugo," originally appeared in *The Nineteenth Century*, July and August, 1885 : the remaining portion, " La Légende des Siècles," in *The Fortnightly Review*, October, 1883.

MISCELLANIES. By ALGERNON CHARLES SWINBURNE. London : Chatto and Windus, 1886, pp. xii. 390.

CONTENTS : Preface ; Short Notes on English Poets ; A Century of English Poetry ; Congreve ; Collins ; Wordsworth and Byron ; Charles Lamb and George Wither ; Landor ; Keats ; Tennyson and Musset ; Emily Brontë ; Charles Reade ; Auguste Vacquerie ; Mary Queen of Scots. APPENDIX I. A Relic of Dryden ; II. Sir Henry Taylor on Shelley ; III. Note on the Character of Mary Queen of Scots.

The Preface and the second division of the Appendix appeared in this volume for the first time : its other contents had already appeared respectively, as elsewhere indicated, in the *Fortnightly Review*, the *Nineteenth Century*, the *Examiner*, the *Athenæum*, the *Gentleman's Magazine*, the Ninth Edition of the *Encyclopædia Britannica*, &c.

John Webster.—*Nineteenth Century*, June, 1886 (vol. xix., pp. 861-881).

The Commonweal. A Song for Unionists.—*Times*, Thursday, July 1, 1886 (fol. 9, col. 5).

Victor Hugo { "Théâtre en Liberté."—*Athenæum*, May 15, 1886. { "La Fin de Satan."—*ib.*, July 10, 1886.

By Twilight. (Eleven lines of verse, divided into three stanzas.)— *Athenæum*, August 21, 1886, p. 240.

The Literary Record of the "Quarterly Review."—Two Letters dated November 1 and 13, 1886, and signed "A. C. Swinburne." —*Athenæum*, November 6 and 20, 1886, pp. 600-601, 671.

In a Garden. (Seven stanzas of four lines each.)—*English Illustrated Magazine*, December, 1886 (vol. iv., pp. 131-132).

Thackeray and Fraser's Magazine.—Two letters dated "The Pines, Putney Hill, Dec. 24, 1880," and "The Pines, July 3, 1886," and signed "A. C. Swinburne."—Printed in the Introduction to *Sultan Stork and other Stories and Sketches by William Makepeace Thackeray. Now first collected.* London : George Redway, 1887 [1886].

1887.

Thomas Dekker. By Algernon Charles Swinburne.—*Nineteenth Century*, January 1887 (vol. xxi., pp. 81-103).

A Ballad of Bath.—*English Illustrated Magazine*, February 1887 (vol. iv., pp. 371-372).

Philip Bourke Marston. Sonnet dated Feb. 15, 1887.—Printed in *The Athenæum*, February 19, 1887, p. 257, in an obituary notice by Mr. Theodore Watts.

Cyril Tourneur.   By Algernon Charles Swinburne.—*Nineteenth Century*, March 1887 (vol. xxi., pp. 415-427).

A WORD FOR THE NAVY.   By ALGERNON CHARLES SWINBURNE. London : George Redway, MDCCCLXXXVII., pp. 16.
Only two hundred and fifty numbered copies issued.   Printed at the Chiswick Press.
This poem contains twelve stanzas of eight lines each.   It was first published in a volume entitled *Sea Song and River Rhyme from Chaucer to Tennyson, selected and edited by Estelle Davenport Adams. With a new poem by Algernon Charles Swinburne.*   London : George Redway, MDCCCLXXXVII., pp. vii-xiii.

The Question.   1887.   (Twenty stanzas of five lines each, signed " Algernon Charles Swinburne.")—*Daily Telegraph*, Friday, April 29, 1887.

A Retrospect.   To the Editor of the *Times.*—Letter dated May 3, and signed " Algernon Charles Swinburne."—*Times*, Friday, May 6, 1887.

Unionism and Crime.—April, 1887.—To the Editor of the *St. James's Gazette.*—Letter signed " A Gladstonite."—*St. James's Gazette*, Friday, May 6, 1887, p. 5.
" We fancy," says an editorial rider following the letter, " that in this ingenious epistle we detect the hand of Mr. Algernon Swinburne."

Mazzini and the Union.   To the Editor of the *Times.*—Letter dated " The Pines, Putney-hill, S.W., May 7," and signed " Algernon Charles Swinburne."—*Times*, Wednesday, May 11, 1887, fol. 14, col. 5.

The Jubilee, 1887.—Fifty stanzas of five lines each, signed "Algernon Charles Swinburne."—*Nineteenth Century*, June 1887 (vol. xxi., pp. 781-791).

CHISWICK PRESS :—C. WHITTINGHAM AND CO., TOOKS COURT,
CHANCERY LANE.